CLASSIC FAIRY TALES

First published in Great Britain in 2007 by Zero To Ten Limited
2A Portman Mansions, Chiltern Street, London W1U 6NR

This edition © 2007 Zero To Ten Limited
© Larousse/S.E.J.E.R 2004
© Larousse/VUEF 2003

British Library Cataloguing in Publication Data:
A CIP catalogue record for this book is available from the British Library.

ISBN-10: 1 84089 468 7
13-digit ISBN (from 1 January 2007) 978 1 84089 468 4
Printed in Malaysia

CLASSIC FAIRY TALES

ZERO TO TEN

CONTENTS

DONKEY SKIN

There was once a grand king who was loved by his people and respected by his neighbours. It could be said he was the most content of all the kings. His happiness increased further when he married a princess as beautiful as she was virtuous, and they lived together in perfect harmony. In time they were blessed with a child, a girl so full of graces and charms everyone was smitten by her.

The palace itself was magnificent and abundantly tasteful. The ministers were wise and skillful, the courtiers were loyal and steadfast, the servants faithful and hardworking, the stables vast and filled with the world's most beautiful horses. However when strangers came to visit these remarkable stables they were surprised to see that the most favoured stable was given not to any of the fine horses but to a female donkey – and not even a good-looking example of a donkey either, for this one had the longest ears anyone had ever seen. What they did not know was nature had created an extraordinary animal here. Each night it did not leave manure in its stall, but gold coins.

However wealth is no protection from the hand of fate and the heavens decreed that the king's wife would fall ill, and there was not a doctor in the land who could help. Death comes to rich and poor alike and all knew that the queen was not long for this world.

Grief swept the kingdom, but none of the good souls there were affected as badly as the poor king. He was devastated at the prospect of losing his dear wife and made offerings and said prayers at every church and temple in the land. His pleas were in vain.

The queen, sensing her final hour drawing near, called for the king who broke down in tears. "Before I die," said the queen, "I ask one thing of you. If you are to remarry…"

At this point the king cried out pitiably and held his wife's hands to his tear-stained face. He did not want to think of marrying again when his true love was dying before him. "No, no!" he cried. "I'd rather die and go with you!"

"The Kingdom," replied the queen with a sudden firmness in her frail voice, "needs a future king. I have only given you a daughter and by the rules of our land she cannot reign. You need a male heir – your people demand it. However, before you choose a new wife promise me that you will only marry someone more beautiful than me. Swear it and I shall die happy."

So why did the queens ask for this? Well, one can only imagine that she did not really want the king to remarry, as she never believed that anyone was as beautiful or as regal as she.

Finally, the queen died. Never before had a husband grieved so much for a wife. He cried and wailed all the day and right through the night.

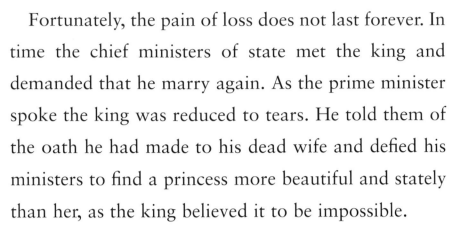

Fortunately, the pain of loss does not last forever. In time the chief ministers of state met the king and demanded that he marry again. As the prime minister spoke the king was reduced to tears. He told them of the oath he had made to his dead wife and defied his ministers to find a princess more beautiful and stately than her, as the king believed it to be impossible.

However, it appeared that the ministers were not as loyal as the king thought. They wanted power for themselves but dared not risk taking the crown by force, fearing the people would rise against them. Instead they wanted the king to resign – and they planned to force him into it. They knew no other princess had the queen's qualities, so they started to plant seeds of worry in the king's mind. What if the king could not find a new wife they said? His daughter would marry a foreign prince who would take over the kingdom. The people may not like this; it might lead to revolution and the ruin of the kingdom. Perhaps the ministers should take over?

The king promised that he would consider his options and keep the ministers informed. He sent out courtiers to find him all of the available princesses from the neighbouring countries. They returned bearing portraits, but none were as regal as his much-missed wife and so the matter remained unresolved.

The ministers were growing impatient so they decided to force the matter. Pretending that they were worried about the future of the kingdom, they said that if no foreign princess could be found he must marry his own daughter! They claimed she was as regal and beautiful as the queen, which was true; but a father can't marry his daughter – it is against all the rules and laws – and they knew that and knew the king would not do it. Would he agree or abdicate? The king explained the situation to his daughter.

She was, as you might expect, horrified by the terrible proposition and begged him to fight the decision.

The king did not need persuading but he still worried about what would happen to the kingdom. He went to seek council with a powerful old druid. However the druid was more ambitious than he was religious and advised the king badly. He told the king that he must either marry the daughter or abdicate.

With a heavy heart the king went back to his daughter and told her they had to marry. It was wrong, so wrong. What could they do?

All the princess could think to do was to seek the comfort of her godmother, the fairy Lilas. That night she harnessed a sheep to a small carriage and set off for the fairy's home.

The fairy was well aware of what was happening in the kingdom but told her beloved goddaughter not to be concerned. All would be well if the princess followed the fairy's instructions to the letter.

"Your father is in a terrible position," said the fairy. "Neither you nor your father can be seen to go against the wishes of the druid or the ministers, so this is what you must do. Say you will marry your father but to satisfy your imagination you must have a dress the very colour of the day. Of course he will not be able to get you such a thing, so you will not have to get married."

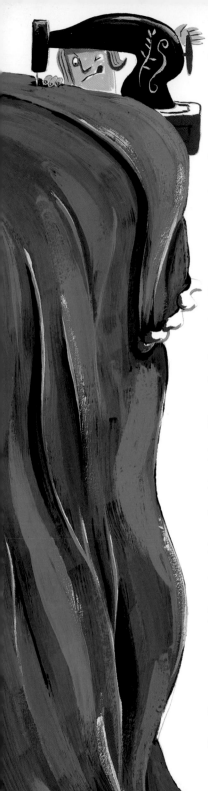

The princess thanked the fairy and returned home. The next morning she explained to her father that she would not marry him without the special dress.

The king assembled the finest tailors in the land. He ordered them to make the special dress and warned them that they would hang if they failed. His threats obviously worked, as he did not have long to wait. Two days later the tailors returned with the desired garment. The heavens themselves could not have produced a more beautiful blue, and through the dress ran threads the colour of golden clouds. The princess was shocked – the dress was the colour of the day itself. She rushed back to see her fairy godmother. She too was surprised by the tailor's ability, but told the princess to ask for a dress the colour of the moon.

The king could refuse his daughter nothing, so once again summoned his tailors and ordered them to make a dress the colour of the moon. Less than twenty four

hours later the tailors delivered the dress, which shone with cold bright light of the moon. Despite the beauty of the dress, all the princess could do was weep when she saw it.

Again the princess went to see Lilas her fairy godmother. "What you should do," said Lilas, "is ask your father for a dress the colour of the sun. Unless I am mistaken, many have tried but none have ever achieved such a feat. If nothing else, it will buy you some time."

The princess asked her father for a dress that shone like the sun and the king immediately ordered it to be made. He gave the jewels from his crown to the tailors who ground them down and sewed the dust into the new dress. When they had finished it glowed so brightly it would have blinded anyone who looked at it for too long. Undoubtedly it was a dress just like the sun.

The dress was the most magnificent thing anyone had ever seen, but that was of no comfort to the princess. She took the dress and rushed to her room in

tears. Soon afterwards her fairy godmother appeared, more ashamed of herself than you can imagine. When she saw the dress she went bright red in anger.

"This is a terrible blow, but we shall not be defeated," cried Lilas. "We must make your father so indignant that he sees sense and calls off this ridiculous marriage! What you should do my dear is ask for something that we know your father will not give you. And I have thought of just the thing. Ask for the skin of his precious donkey – the one that produces all the gold coins."

The princess was relieved to hear that the fairy could think of another way out of this detestable marriage; and she went to her father and told him that she wanted the donkey's skin before she would marry him.

Though the king was taken aback by the request and worried about the fate of his kingdom, he had the donkey slaughtered and the skin brought to the young princess. Now the girl was desperately worried and ran back to her chambers and called for her fairy

godmother. The fairy arrived at once. "My poor dear child," she said when the princess arrived on her doorstep, her hair wild and face streaked with tears. "There is only one thing left to do, you must flee. You are sacrificing all to protect your virtue and the gods will look favourably on that. Wrap yourself in the donkey's skin – do not take it off – and go as far as you can. I shall cast a spell so your clothes will follow you underground. I also give you this wand. If you should need any of your possessions just tap the wand on the ground. Now go and delay no further."

The princess slipped out of her rooms and left the palace she had called home under the cover of the ink-black night. When it was noticed that the princess was gone there was uproar in the palace. The king felt the loss of his daughter as much of that of his wife.

He immediately dispatched as many men as could be spared to try and find her. Though his army spread out across the countryside like a plague of locusts, the good fairy cast a spell that made the princess invisible to the king's search party.

So the princess went further from the palace than she had even been, even by carriage, into a new kingdom. On the way she begged for food, which people were happy to give her, but no

one would take her in, as she looked so dirty.

However when the princess drew near to a beautiful city she noticed a farm. The farmer's wife told her that she was looking for someone to wash clothes, take care of the turkeys and sheep and slop out the pigs. Taking the princess for a typical traveller, the farmer's wife offered the princess the job.

The princess, weary from travelling and sleeping outside, gratefully accepted it.

The woman took the princess into the kitchen where she started work immediately. The other farm workers all came to look at her and laugh at her appearance, wrapped as she was in a filthy donkey skin.

Over time the other workers grew used to the princess' appearance and the cruel jibes ceased. Furthermore the girl was so conscientious and hard-working that the farmer's wife made sure she came to no harm. The princess cleaned everything so it shone and was so good at caring for the animals you would think she had been doing it all her life.

One day as the princess sat by a pond thinking over her situation, she happened to glance at her reflection. For the first time the princess saw herself as others saw her – covered in dirt and wearing a filthy donkey skin. She furiously washed her hands and face and soon her skin gleamed as white as ivory. Overjoyed with the transformation she stripped off the donkey skin and plunged into the pond to get washed. Of course she had to put the skin back on to return to the farm; but the princess knew the next day was a holiday so she could use Lilas' wand to summon her clothes and wear a dress again.

The next day the princess tapped the wand on the floor and the clothes appeared. She dressed; the room was so small the train of the dress could not open

fully, but the princess did not mind. She brushed her hair and put diamonds in it. It was such a relief to look like a princess again that she promised herself that she would do this every holiday and Sunday, even it were only the sheep and the turkeys which could see her like this.

One holiday, as the princess changed into the dress the colour of the sun, the son of the king who ruled this kingdom arrived. He owned this farm and had stopped here to rest on his way home from hunting.

Now the prince was a good-looking young man, intelligent and strong; as loved by his people, as he was adored by his parents. He gladly accepted a light meal, and then had a good look around the farmhouse.

By and by he walked down a dark corridor and came to a door that was locked. Curious to know what lay behind the door he peered through the keyhole and saw the beautiful princess. Her dress was so splendid and she looked so regal and yet modest that he thought her to be some kind of goddess. He was absolutely smitten by this beautiful stranger.

He was sorry to leave the dark corridor but the prince was determined to find out who it was behind the locked door. When he asked at the farmhouse everyone laughed and told him that it was just a traveller they called Donkey Skin because of the animal pelt she wore. They had only taken her in because they felt sorry for the dirty-looking creature and it was her job to look after the animals.

The prince was hardly satisfied with this explanation, but realised that the farm hands could shed no more light on the situation, and that it was useless to question them further.

He returned to his father's palace absolutely and deeply in love. He could think of nothing else but the mysterious girl behind the locked door. He resolved to return to the farmhouse and find out who she was – even if it meant breaking down the door.

However that night the prince was struck down by a fever brought on by falling so intensely in love. He was so ill he nearly died.

The prince was an only child and the queen was desperately worried by his condition. She summoned the best doctors in the kingdom and offered a huge reward for curing her son; but despite their best efforts his condition did not improve.

What they did notice was that he seemed to be suffering from some terrible sorrow. The queen implored her son to tell her what was wrong. Did he want to be king? His father would gladly give up the throne for him. Was he in love? They would get the girl for him even if it were the princess of a king who his father was at war with. And all the time the queen spoke the ears ran from her face and dropped onto her son the prince.

"Madame," replied the prince in a weak voice, "I am not driven by desire for the throne. I hope that my father will see many more summers as king of our land and I will be his most faithful of subjects for as long as he reigns. As to a wife, I have no thoughts of marrying yet mother, but I will always obey you no matter what the personal cost to myself."

"Oh my son," replied the queen, "I shall spare no expense in finding a cure for you; for if you die then your father and I shall surely die from grief."

"Mother, I shall not be responsible for the death of two people who are so dear to me," said the prince. "I desire that Donkey Skin makes a cake and that it is brought to me as soon as it is complete."

As you might imagine the queen thought his request was a little odd and demanded to know who Donkey Skin was.

"She is a most unpleasant creature, nearly as bad as a wolf," one of the guards told the queen. "She dresses

in a filthy donkey skin and looks after the animals on one of your son's farms."

"What she looks like is unimportant," replied the queen. "The prince must have eaten some of her baking at some point. It is no doubt the ravings of an ill boy, but get this Donkey Skin to make him a cake."

Soldiers were sent immediately to the farm to find Donkey Skin and order her to make a cake for the prince. Now, some people believe that when the prince spied upon her through the keyhole the princess had noticed that someone was looking and had peered through her window to see the prince as he left. Although she did not know exactly who he was, she guessed who he might be. Whatever the truth of the matter, Donkey Skin was happy that the prince knew who she was. She locked herself in her room, took off the donkey skin, washed, and put on a silver coloured

corset and skirt. She then set to work baking a cake. However, unknown to her, as she stirred the ingredients a ring she wore fell into the mix. When the cake was baked to perfection the princess pulled on the filthy donkey skin and took the cake to the waiting soldiers. As she handed the cake over she asked how the prince was, but the soldiers ignored her, took the cake and sped back to the palace.

When the soldiers arrived the prince greedily snatched the cake from their hands and started wolfing it down as fast as he could. In fact, he was eating it so quickly he nearly choked to death. He coughed up the object that had stuck in his throat, and discovered it was a ring. No ordinary ring

either; the prince noted that it was set with a beautiful emerald and the band was of such a delicate gold he imagined it would fit only the prettiest finger in the land. He kissed the ring a thousand times and hid it under his pillow; every so often he would take it out and gaze at it when he thought no one was looking. And yet he did not to ask to see Donkey Skin. How could he tell people of what he had seen through the keyhole? They would laugh at him and tell him he was dreaming. He fell into his fevered state yet again. The doctors were so perplexed that all they

could think was that he was lovesick, and if the cause was not found soon, he would most probably die. The king and queen rushed to his bedside imploring him, "Tell us who the girl is and we give you our blessing for you to marry her – we don't care if she is a princess or a serving girl."

The prince was moved by the kind words of his parents. He turned to them and said: "I do not wish to marry anyone you do not approve of," he said, "and to prove it, look at this." He showed his parents the ring he kept under his pillow. "I will marry the woman whose finger fits this ring," the prince continued. "And judging by the size and craftsmanship of the ring I don't think it belongs to any serving girl."

The king and queen inspected the ring and agreed that the owner must be from an exceedingly wealthy family. The king was overjoyed that his son would be marrying into a good family, being a bit old-fashioned on that front. He ordered that messengers be sent with drums and trumpets all over the kingdom to announce that every lady should come to the palace to try the ring. Whoever it fitted would marry the heir to the throne.

First the princesses arrived, and then the duchesses, then the marchionesses and finally the baronesses; but the emerald ring did not fit a single one of them. Every woman of noble birth had come to the palace and as attractive as they were, none was able to get their finger into the small gold band. The prince, whose fever had abated, watched all this with dismay. When everyone had tried he called for every cook, cleaner or shepherdess to come and try. They duly came and duly went, as the ring did not fit any of them either.

"Has the one called Donkey Skin – the one who made the cake – come yet?" asked the prince.

Everyone burst out laughing at the very thought of such a filthy creature trying on the ring.

"No one is excluded from this search!" boomed the king. "Fetch her at once!"

So off went the messengers to find her, laughing all the way. The princess heard the sound of trumpets and drums and knew it was due to her lost ring – she knew that everyone had been to the palace to try on a mystery ring. She loved the prince and had been worried that some other girl would have a finger thin enough to fit the emerald ring. Hearing the noise

outside confirmed to her that her fears had not been realised. She quickly washed herself – you need clean hands to try on such a ring after all – and then put on her beautiful silver skirt and corset. When the messenger arrived at her door she threw on the donkey skin and went off to the palace. When she

arrived everyone laughed again at the thought of such an unusual and dirty girl marrying the heir to the throne. When the prince himself set eyes on her he could not believe that she could possibly be the girl he was looking for. The thought of marrying a girl like this did not please him, but he had to find out if the ring fitted her. Tired and confused he said to the princess, "So you live on the farm that lies at the very edge of our fine city; in your room at the end of a dark corridor?" She nodded.

"Show me your hand," he said with a deep sigh.

Can you imagine the surprise that swept around the palace when a clean, delicate hand stretched from beneath the dirty donkey skin? Can you picture the shock the people felt when the ring slipped easily onto

one of the girl's dainty fingers? Bit by bit the princess shrugged off the donkey skin she had worn in public for so long. To the great joy and relief of the prince (and his parents) a beautiful girl now stood in front of him. The prince felt weak at the knees but did not fall because the king and queen had thrown their arms around him to congratulate him on finding such a suitable bride.

The princess was also overcome by such a display of love and happiness, but could not think what to say. However at that moment the ceiling opened and her fairy godmother, Lilas, appeared. She told the assembled people of the court all about the princess and how she came to be here. The king and queen were thrilled to hear that the girl their son was to marry was in fact a princess. The prince, too, was pleased, but would not have cared if she had been a serving girl so captivated was he by her beauty. The prince was so impatient to get married that he would gladly have done it there and then with no festivities.

The princess, however, held him in her arms and told him that she could not get married without the blessing of her father. There had to be a proper ceremony and the first person to be invited had to be Lilas, as she had helped her so much.

Kings and queens from countries far and near came to the wedding. Some in sedans, some in carriages and the ones from further afield arrived on elephants, tigers and eagles. But the grandest entrance of all was by the father of the princess. This noble king had married a beautiful queen who was a widow herself. When father, daughter and stepmother met they threw their arms around each and wept for joy. The prince's parents presented their son to the king and he was pleased to see that he was a fine and noble man – a son-in-law he could be proud of. Both families were joined in mutual respect and love.

The wedding was a grand affair, which fitted the situation perfectly. The crowds cheered and the family smiled and wept, but through it all the happy couple remained modest and attentive, which made the people love them even more.

That same day the prince's father gave up his throne and the boy became king. He proved so wise and just that all his subjects admired him. In fact the happy couple reigned together for over a hundred years and their love did not diminish one bit through their long and happy lives.

RICKY WITH THE TUFT

There was once a Queen who gave birth to a son so ugly that many people wondered if he was even human. However a fairy smiled upon the poor baby that day and said it would be a well-natured child and would be blessed with an uncommon amount of good sense. She added that as part of her gift the boy would be able to bestow some of his good sense on whomever he loved the most.

This was some comfort to the poor queen. It was true that that as soon as the child could talk he said a thousand wonderful things and in everything he did there was a sense and intelligence that was quite charming. Oh, and I forgot to say that he came into the world with a little tuft of hair on its head so they called him "Ricky with the tuft" because Richard was the family name.

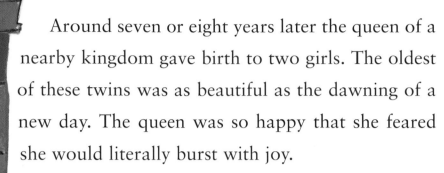

Around seven or eight years later the queen of a nearby kingdom gave birth to two girls. The oldest of these twins was as beautiful as the dawning of a new day. The queen was so happy that she feared she would literally burst with joy.

The fairy, which was at the birth of Ricky with the tuft, was also present here. In order to stop the queen getting carried away or being big-headed the fairy pronounced that the queen's beautiful child would be as stupid as she was pretty and completely lacking in any common sense. The queen was horrified, but she soon felt worse for her second daughter turned out to be exceedingly ugly.

"Do not worry Madam," said the fairy. "As compensation, your younger daughter will have so much sense she will not mind her lack of beauty."

"I hope to God you're right," said the queen. "But is there no way of making my elder daughter any brighter?"

"No, I'm afraid not," replied the fairy. "However, I give her a gift – she can make the person whom she likes the most as good looking as she is."

As the princesses grew up, so their gifts grew with them. Everyone, but everyone, talked about the eldest's beauty and the youngest's great sense. Mind you their defects also grew with them, too. Everyone also commented on this, mentioning the youngest's fearsome ugliness and the eldest's rank stupidity. Not only was the older sister stupid, but she was also hugely clumsy and could not be trusted to carry – or even be near – anything that was remotely fragile.

Even the simple act of having a drink was beyond her. Inevitably most of the liquid would end up on her clothes as she somehow managed to miss her mouth whilst taking a sip.

Although beauty can be a huge advantage in life, it turned out the younger princess was the most favoured in company. Of course people would initially flock to the beautiful sister but would soon tire of her stupidity. Then they would be attracted, like moths to a flame, to the younger sister with her wit and entertaining conversation. Within a quarter of an hour the elder would be left alone and the younger crowded by admirers.

Even the elder sister wasn't so stupid that she didn't realise what was going on. She would gladly have

been half as beautiful if she could only have been half as intelligent as her sister. Although the queen realised this she still could not stop herself chiding her elder daughter for her stupidity and this served only to make the princess feel even worse about life.

One day when the beautiful princess was hiding away in the woods, as she liked to do, she spotted a well-dressed, though outrageously ugly, man coming towards her. It was Prince Ricky with the tuft. He had seen a portrait of the beautiful sister, had fallen in love and had left his father's kingdom to come looking for her. Being a bright lad, he had found her, too. He was overjoyed to see that she was alone. He went over and introduced himself. However, seeing how sad she looked he was moved to say,

"I do not understand how a woman so beautiful can look so sad. I have met many pretty ladies, but none, not one, was nearly as beautiful as you."

"If you say so," replied the princess, but said no more.

"Beauty," said Ricky with the tuft, "is such a great advantage it must outrank all other gifts. As you possess such a gift I can't possibly see what it is that afflicts you."

"I would rather," replied the princess, "be as ugly as you but have more sense, than be as beautiful as I am and as useless as I am."

"There is nothing," said Ricky, "that marks one out

as having intelligence as to not believe that one possesses it. The more one has of it, the more one wants."

"I don't know anything about that," replied the princess, "but I do know that I have the brains of a chicken and it upsets me greatly."

"If that is all that troubles you," said the prince, "then I can solve that in a moment."

"How?" asked the princess.

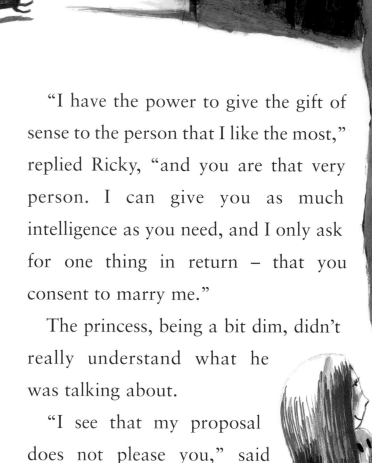

"I have the power to give the gift of sense to the person that I like the most," replied Ricky, "and you are that very person. I can give you as much intelligence as you need, and I only ask for one thing in return – that you consent to marry me."

The princess, being a bit dim, didn't really understand what he was talking about.

"I see that my proposal does not please you," said Ricky. "In which case I shall give you one full year in which to think about it."

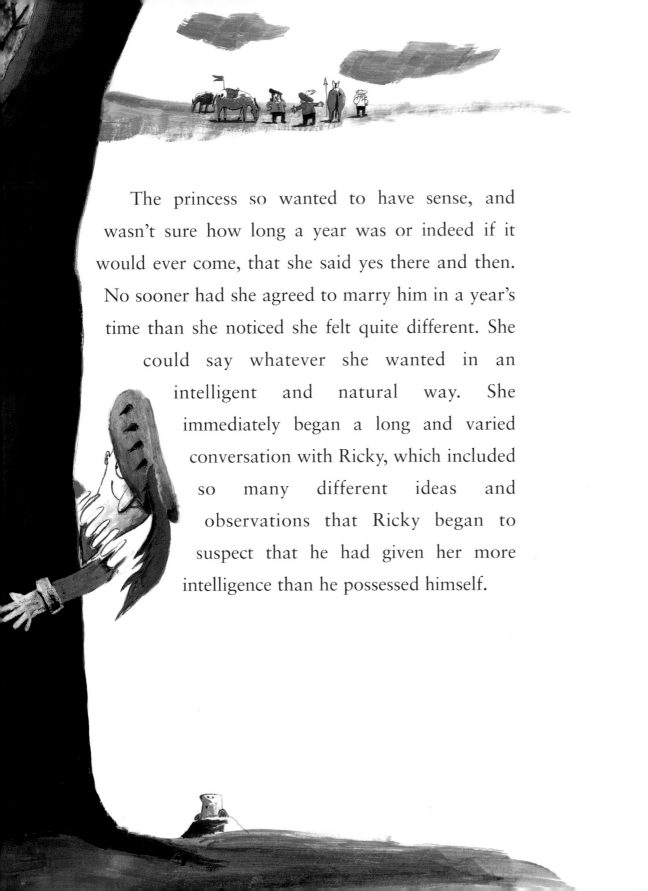

The princess so wanted to have sense, and wasn't sure how long a year was or indeed if it would ever come, that she said yes there and then. No sooner had she agreed to marry him in a year's time than she noticed she felt quite different. She could say whatever she wanted in an intelligent and natural way. She immediately began a long and varied conversation with Ricky, which included so many different ideas and observations that Ricky began to suspect that he had given her more intelligence than he possessed himself.

When she returned to the palace everyone noticed the extraordinary change that had come over the elder princess. Whereas before they had heard only clueless ramblings they now heard her talking in an intelligent and incisive manner. The whole palace was ecstatically happy. The king would ask her advice now and held court in her rooms. The only person it did not please was the younger princess. Now her sister had brains as well as beauty she was no longer the centre of attention. She was just the ugly sister once more.

The news of the transformation spread far and wide. Soon eligible young princes were beating a path to the elder sister's door. Over the next year they all asked for her hand in marriage, but she turned them down, none of them having enough sense for her liking.

However one arrived who was so rich, intelligent and good-looking that she could not help falling for him. The king noticed this. It was the custom at that time for a girl's father to choose who his daughter would marry. However the king was a sensible kind of chap and told his daughter that she had the right to choose her own husband. She thanked him and asked for time to think about things.

She went for a walk in the woods to mull things over – by chance the very same woods in which she had met Ricky with the tuft. While she was walking she heard a noise that sounded like lots of people running backwards and forwards beneath her feet.

Listening carefully she could hear voices.

"Bring me the pot," said one

"Give me the kettle," said another.

"The fire needs wood," said another.

The ground opened up and there was a huge kitchen with all the cooks, waiters and pageboys necessary for a grand feast. Up came twenty or thirty cooks each carrying a roasted hog. They took them to a long table in the woods, all the while singing a merry work song.

The princess was astounded and asked them what they were doing.

"This," said a cook with a flourish of his arm, "is for Prince Ricky with the tuft. He is to be married tomorrow."

This came as such a surprise to the princess it made her feel all faint. At once she remembered the promise she made to Ricky before he had given her his great gift; and at the same time she realised to her horror that the year was nearly up.

She continued on her way but had not gone more than thirty paces when Ricky with the tuft himself appeared. He was dressed in the fine robes of a man who was about to be married.

"You see," said he, "just as promised, I have returned. And I have no doubt that you have returned to me to give me your hand and make me the happiest man alive."

"I must tell you," replied the princess, "that I have yet to be resolved on this matter and fear that my decision will most probably not be the one you want to hear."

"I am astounded, Madame," said Ricky with the tuft.

"I can believe it," replied the princess. "But if I did this to a brutal man, or one with no sense, I would be highly troubled. He would say, 'A princess should keep her word and you must marry me as you promised.' However the man to whom I talk is gifted with great intelligence and reason. You knew me when I had only beauty, and no sense. I did not understand what marriage meant, and if I did not understand something how could I agree to it? If you really wanted to make me your wife you should have left me as the stupid creature you found rather than allow me to see things as clearly as I do."

"If a man of no reason can be upset," said Ricky, "then surely I should be allowed the same freedom, especially as this is over a matter of my own personal happiness. Is it reasonable or rational that a man of wit and intelligence can be denied, leaving him at a disadvantage when compared to a man who has none of these gifts? Can you pretend this, you who have wished for and got such wit and intelligence yourself? Apart from my ugliness, what is it about me that so displeases you? Am I not intelligent enough for you? Do I lack manners?"

"By no means," replied the princess. "You are abundant in those virtues."

"If that is true then I am happy," said Ricky with the tuft, "for that means that it is within your power to make me the happiest man alive."

"How is that?" asked the princess.

"If you want it to be so, it can be so," said Ricky. "The fairy who, on the day of my birth, gave me the ability to give the gift of intelligence to whoever I loved gave a similar gift to you on your birth. You are able to make whoever you desire more handsome."

"If that is true," said the princess, "then I wish with all my heart that you are turned into the most beautiful man in the whole world, and I make it my gift to you as you did for me."

No sooner had the princess uttered these words than Ricky with the tuft was transformed. He became the most handsome man the princess had ever seen.

Was it the gift that the fairy gave which worked this magic, or was it, as some suppose, to be the work of love? Well the truth of the matter is that the princess had looked into her heart of hearts and had ignored the ugliness without and seen the beauty within Ricky of the tuft.

His hump she now took to be broad shoulders, his limp she found charming.

His squint had not hidden from her his sparkling eyes and his large red nose had seemed positively heroic.

That is not to say, of course, that she wasn't mightily impressed with the changes in our lovelorn prince as a result of the magic spell.

What was a girl to do? Marry this good-looking prince, I hear you cry, and that dear reader is exactly what she did. A promise is a promise after all, and some promises are easier to keep than others. The king was overjoyed with his new son-in-law and the two newly-weds were as happy as they had ever dared hoped they could be.

BEAUTY AND THE BEAST

There was once a rich merchant who had six children; three girls and three boys. The merchant believed a good education was the way to get on in the world and so ensured his children had the best teachers possible.

His daughters were all good looking, but the youngest was the prettiest. Even as a baby her beauty was obvious and she was called Beautiful Child – Beauty for short – a name that made her other siblings jealous. Not only was she better looking, but Beauty was also a better person than her sisters, who were rude and spiteful. They spent their days dressing up and going to parties. They sneered at those with less money than themselves and refused to talk to anyone they considered inferior. And they mocked Beauty for

reading books instead of partying and gossiping.

As it was well known that the daughters were rich and well educated, many merchants asked them to be their wives. The elder girls just laughed and said that they could never marry a tradesman, and that only a duke – or at the very least a count – would do. Beauty on the other hand, thanked her suitors but gently said no. She was too young, she said, and needed to be at home to keep her father company.

Then one day the merchant lost his fortune when his business did badly. All that he had left was a small country house many miles from the city. He told his children that they could live there, but they would have to work like peasants to survive. The older sisters were horrified. Work? They would rather get married, and there were people who would take them even without their riches.

The sisters were wrong. With no wealth the ladies had lost their appeal – a result of their years of rudeness.

"They don't deserve any sympathy!" The people said. "It's about time that they were brought down to earth – and nothing does that better than looking after sheep."

But at the same time they also said:

"Poor Beauty, how unfair it is on her. She was always so kind to the poor people and she's so honest, too."

There were a number of gentlemen who still wanted to marry her, even though she was poor. Although Beauty was flattered, she turned them all down, telling them that it would be unfair to abandon her father in his misfortune and that she would go with him to the country to help out in whatever way she could.

 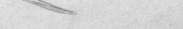

When they arrived at their new home in the country the merchant and his children set about tending the fields. Beauty woke at four each morning to clean the house and prepare breakfast for the family. At first she did not enjoy her new life, working harder than her servants used to; but as time went on she got used to it. She grew stronger and did not tire so easily, and began to find time to read again, or play the harpsichord.

Her sisters, on the other hand, were bored to tears. They got up at ten and wandered about dreaming of their beautiful clothes and rich friends.

"Look at our little sister;" they said to each other, "she's so stupid she's actually happy in this dreadful place."

The good merchant did not think of his youngest daughter in the same way that his other daughters did. He knew it was her who cleaned the house. He also knew that it was her good nature that made her the most attractive of his offspring.

After a year had passed the merchant received a letter telling him one of his ships, laden with goods, had arrived in port. The news was of interest to the elder sisters too – perhaps this meant that they could finally leave the countryside. When it was time for their father to leave to sell his goods the elder sisters told him to bring them back new dresses and hats. Beauty, on the other hand, asked for nothing and in truth did not think their father's profits would allow him to buy all the things her sisters wanted.

"You have not asked me for anything," the merchant said to Beauty. "What would you like?"

"As you are kind enough to ask," replied Beauty, "then please bring me back a rose – they don't grow here."

Beauty really did not care whether she had a rose or not, but she felt that she had to ask for something so that she did not show up her older, greedier sisters.

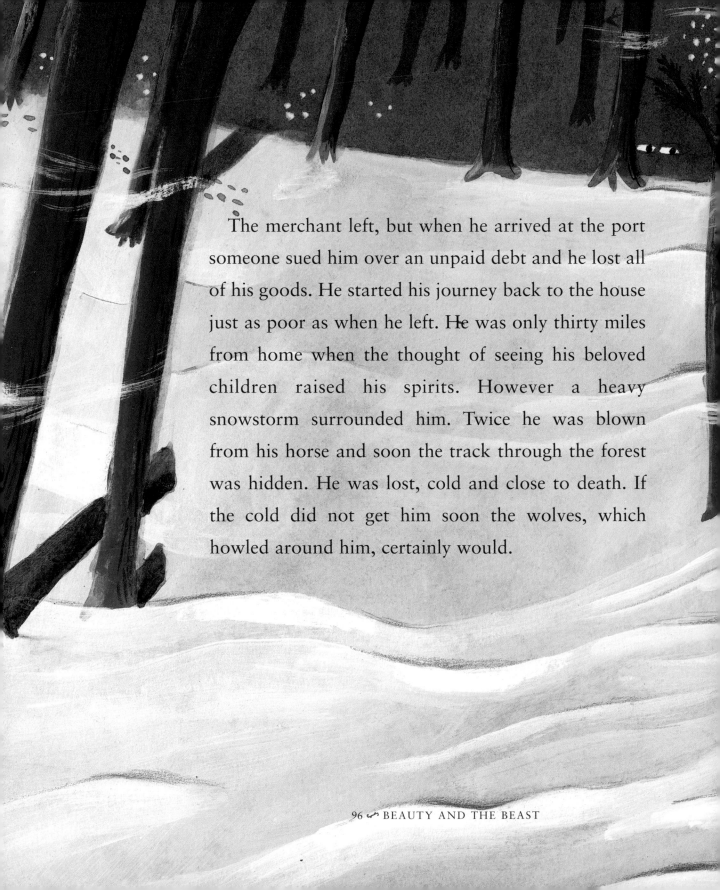

The merchant left, but when he arrived at the port someone sued him over an unpaid debt and he lost all of his goods. He started his journey back to the house just as poor as when he left. He was only thirty miles from home when the thought of seeing his beloved children raised his spirits. However a heavy snowstorm surrounded him. Twice he was blown from his horse and soon the track through the forest was hidden. He was lost, cold and close to death. If the cold did not get him soon the wolves, which howled around him, certainly would.

At that moment the merchant saw, down a long avenue of trees, a bright light in the distance. He headed towards the light and realised it came from the windows of a large palace. The merchant thanked God for such a stroke of luck, but his happiness turned to puzzlement when he reached the gates of the palace. The gates were open but it seemed that no one was about. He spotted some stables close by, so led his horse – which was half-dead from hunger – inside. There were hay and oats aplenty here and the horse greedily tucked in. The merchant tied up his mount and headed for the palace. Again the door was open but no one was about. He entered a room and found a blazing fire and a table, set for one, laden with fine foods.

As the weather had chilled him to the bone the merchant sought out the heat of the fire. "Surely the owner of this house or his servants won't begrudge me making myself comfortable after all I've been through," thought the merchant. "Someone must come by soon so I can explain." However time crept by and come eleven o'clock no one had arrived. He could resist the food no more and swiftly gobbled up a chicken and drank some wine. Thus emboldened he set off to explore the palace. He walked through many magnificent rooms until he reached a comfortable-looking bedroom. Noticing that it was after midnight he lay on the bed and fell asleep.

The merchant awoke the next morning at ten and was surprised to see a new set of clothes at the foot of his bed to replace his own that had been ruined by both poverty and the storm.

"Surely the owner of this house has taken pity on me," thought the merchant. He looked out of the window and saw that the snow had gone and outside were beautiful gardens. He went downstairs into the room he had eaten in the night before. Now the table had been re-laid.

"And look," he said, "they have even given me breakfast!"

After eating the merchant made his way down to the stable to fetch his horse. He passed beneath a large rose bush and remembered that Beauty had asked him to bring her back a rose. There were so many here taking one surely wouldn't matter?

At that precise moment the merchant heard a terrible roar – a huge and ferocious monster stood behind him.

"So that is how you show your gratitude?" roared the monster. "I save your life by opening up my palace to you and in return you take my roses, my precious roses. For such ungratefulness you shall die. I give you fifteen minutes to make your peace with God."

The merchant fell on his knees and begged the monster:

"Please excuse me sir, I did not mean to cause offence. I was only taking a rose back to one of my daughters as she requested."

"I am not called Sir," said the monster, "but Beast. I am immune to flattery so do not try. I speak as I see and prefer if others do the same. So you have daughters you say? Well then, I shall pardon you and spare your life if one of your daughters comes here to die instead. Now no discussion – just go! And if one of your daughters refuses to come then you must swear to return yourself within three months."

The merchant had no intention of sacrificing one of his daughters, but he welcomed the opportunity to embrace them for one last time. He was just about to leave when Beast said: "Wait. I do not want you to leave empty-handed. In the room where you slept is a large trunk. You can fill it with whatever you like as long as you can carry it home."

Beast left. The merchant thought: "Well, if I have to die, at least I will have the consolation of leaving bread for my poor children."

He returned to the room where he had been sleeping. Indeed there was a chest as Beast said there would be. When the merchant looked around the room he discovered a huge quantity of gold, which he loaded into the chest. He then retrieved his horse from the stables and set off for his house, happy to be going home rich, but burdened by the terrible fate that awaited him. Before he knew it he was at his little house. His children swarmed around him, but their hugs just set him off crying. He held in his hand a bunch of roses, which he gave to his youngest daughter. "These are for you Beauty. A simple gift but it comes at such a high price." And he proceeded to tell them of what had gone before.

When they heard the merchant's tale the two older girls burst into tears and began to insult Beauty. She on the other hand did not cry.

"How typical," the elder sisters said. "She can't just ask for dresses like us, no, she has to be different and ask for a flower. And now that our father is going to die, she doesn't even cry. She is heartless!"

"What would be the point of crying," replied Beauty. "Father will not die. The monster will accept one of his daughters so I shall go instead. I will happily die in his place to show how great my love for our father is."

"No sister," said Beauty's brothers, "you will not go. We shall find this monster and kill it – or die trying!"

"Alas there is no hope for us, my children," said the merchant. "Beast is too strong to kill. I am overwhelmed by Beauty's kind-hearted gesture, but I

will not allow her to die. My life will only be slightly shorter if I die now and it has been a full life because of you, my dear children."

"No," said Beauty, "you will not return to that palace without me: you cannot stop me from following you. Although young, I am not so attached to life that I would not prefer for the monster to eat me than to live the rest of my life without you."

When she had finished her heartfelt speech Beauty wanted to leave for the palace there and then – if only to escape the obvious wrath of her jealous sisters who could never have imagined such selfless thoughts.

The merchant had been so preoccupied by the conversation that he had forgotten all about the trunk filled with gold. When he went to his room to lie down he saw it there at the foot of his bed. He decided not to tell his children for the older sisters would want to go back to the city, and he had resolved to die in the countryside. Instead he told only Beauty, who in turn told her father that two gentlemen had come during his absence to ask to marry the two other daughters. Beauty had spoken so highly of her sisters that the men had forgiven their selfish ways.

When the time came for the merchant and Beauty to leave, the sisters pretended to cry by holding raw onions to their eyes. The brothers were genuine in their grief, but the merchant was inconsolable at the thought of taking his favourite child to such a terrible place. Beauty did not cry, not wishing to upset anyone any further.

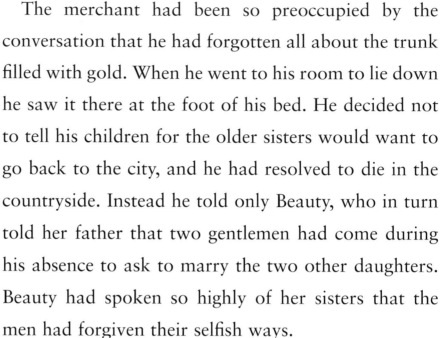

The horse followed the path through the forest and by evening came upon the palace as it had the first time. The horse took itself to the stable while Beauty and her father entered the palace. There they found a magnificent table set for two people to eat. The merchant did not have the stomach for it, but Beauty, with quiet determination, sat down and ate. "If Beast wants to fatten me up I'll make sure I make a decent meal," she thought.

After she had finished her supper Beauty and her father heard a loud noise. The merchant with tears in his eyes bid his daughter farewell as he realised it was Beast arriving. Beauty could not help but tremble when she saw the monster. Beast asked the merchant if Beauty had a good heart. With a quiver in his voice, the merchant replied that she did.

"You have done well," said Beast. "You must leave first thing tomorrow; and I warn you never to return to this place again. Say your goodbyes to your daughter!"

"I shall," said the merchant and Beast left.

"Oh my daughter," said the merchant as he held in his trembling arms, "you must go, leave me here to face Beast."

"No father," replied Beauty. "You must give me up and pray that those in heaven will take pity on me."

They retired to their beds, neither believing that they would rest. However, no sooner had their heads hit their pillows than they were asleep. During the night Beauty dreamt of a lady who said to her:

"I am pleased that you have a good heart, Beauty. Your brave decision to take your father's place shall be rewarded."

When she awoke Beauty told her father of her dream. Though it comforted him slightly it still did not stop him from howling with grief when it was time for them to part.

When the merchant had gone, Beauty sat in the middle of her room and cried. However she was a brave soul, and after a quick prayer resolved not waste any of her time left on earth. Believing Beast would eat her that evening she decided to explore as much of the palace as possible.

Despite the death sentence hanging over her, Beauty was struck by the impressive palace with its well-proportioned rooms and graceful design. She then came upon a door marked "Room of Beauty". She opened the door and was immediately dazzled by the magnificence within. There was a grand library, and a music area with harpsichord and sheet music. "If only I were not to die tonight I could have spent many happy hours here," she thought. She wandered over to the books and pulled out one on which was written in gold letters: 'Your wish is my command: you are both queen and mistress'. "Alas!" sighed Beauty. "All I wish for is to see my poor father to know how he is."

To her surprise the front cover of the book turned into a mirror and on it appeared her father. He was at home looking as sad as it is possible to be. Her elder sisters appeared before him and despite the fact they were trying to look upset Beauty could tell that they were overjoyed to have got rid of her. Then she saw her sisters married and her brothers in the army before everything disappeared and the book was just a book again. However, Beauty could not rid herself of the image of her poor, ill father.

At midday Beauty had an excellent lunch in the same room as before. Beautiful music was playing, but she could see no one about. That evening Beauty again took her place at the table. When she heard the sound of Beast arriving she could not help but tremble.

"Beauty," said the monster, "do you mind if I join you for supper?"

"You are the master," replied Beauty, still trembling.

"No," replied Beast, "I do not want to be here uninvited. If my presence here disturbs you say so and I will go. Now tell me, you find me ugly don't you?"

"That is true," replied Beauty, "I cannot lie. But I believe you to be a good person inside."

"You are right," said Beast, "but I have no sense, no wit. I am just Beast."

"You are not a beast," replied Beauty. "And to think you don't have personality, well that's just wrong."

"Eat Beauty," said Beast. "I shall do you no harm. I only wish for you to be content."

"You are very kind," replied Beauty. "I am content that you have a heart. This makes me think that you are not so ugly after all."

"Yes, yes," said Beast, "I have a good heart, but I am still a monster!"

"I know some people who are bigger monsters than you," replied Beauty. "And I like you better with your monstrous appearance than those who look like men but lie, cheat and steal."

"If I had spirit your words would make me feel better," said Beast, "but I do not. I thank you for your compliment, anyway."

Beauty finished her supper and no longer felt afraid of the terrible monster. However, she was shocked when Beast said: "Beauty, will you marry me?"

Beauty sat for a while without saying anything, mainly because she was afraid of angering Beast by refusing his proposal. Finally, with a quiver in her voice said: "No, Beast."

She waited for an angry response, but Beast merely let out a deep sigh, which seeped through all the corridors of the palace. He looked at her sadly for a moment then said: "Good night, Beauty," then stood up and slowly walked out of the room. Beauty felt great sympathy for Beast. "How unfortunate," she thought, "how something so ugly can be so good."

Beauty spent the next three months living at the palace and life was peaceful enough. Each evening at supper Beast would come and sit with Beauty and they would talk of many things. Each evening Beauty would find out more about Beast. He was such a kind person that she no longer feared him at all. In fact she looked forward to his visits and waited impatiently until nine o'clock, the usual time he came to see her each night.

There was only one thing that upset Beauty about these meetings. Each night, before he left, Beast would ask her to marry him. Beauty always said no and Beast always looked devastated by the response. One night Beauty said to him:

"Beast, you distress me so. If only my heart would allow me to marry you, but I do not love you. You are my dearest friend, but that is all. Can you not be content with that?"

"I respect your honesty," replied Beast. "I know that I am horrible, but I also love you. I will be happy enough if you stay here with me for ever."

Beauty blushed at these words. However, she knew that her father was ill – she had seen him on the magical book – and she wanted to see him again.

"I will stay with you," said Beauty, "but I need to know how my father is. I will die from the pain of not knowing if you refuse me."

"It is better that I die myself," said Beast, "than to cause you a moment of pain. Go to your father. I shall stay here and die."

"No!" said Beauty crying. "I love you too much to want you to die. I promise to return in eight days. You showed me that my sisters are married and that my brothers are in the army. Now my father is all alone. Please allow me to spend a week with him."

"You shall be there tomorrow morning," said Beast. "But remember your promise. When you want to come back lay your ring upon the table before you sleep. Farewell Beauty."

Beast sighed when he said this, as he always did and Beauty went to bed that night upset at the distress she caused him. However, when she woke the next morning she was in her own little bed in her father's house.

The merchant nearly died of joy when he saw his daughter and they held each other in a huge embrace for a quarter of an hour.

Beauty thought that she might not have anything to wear, but the maid said that there was a trunk in her room filled with beautiful dresses trimmed with diamonds. Beauty thanked Beast in her head for his thoughtfulness. She took the plainest dresses and asked the maid to give the others to her sisters. No sooner had the words left her mouth than the trunk disappeared. Her father told her that Beast wanted Beauty to have everything and not to share his gifts to her. When Beauty agreed the trunk reappeared.

While Beauty got dressed news of her arrival reached her sisters, who came running with their husbands. Both of Beauty's sisters were unhappy. The eldest had married a gentleman whom she loved but he only had eyes for himself. He was so vain he looked at himself in the mirror from the moment he got up until he went to bed. The other sister married a man of great energy but who used it to annoy everybody – including his wife. The sisters nearly died of envy when they saw Beauty in a dress fit for a princess and looking more beautiful than ever.

Nothing could stifle their jealousy, which only increased when Beauty told them of her happy life. The two older sisters went down into the garden and wept with frustration.

"How come she's happier than us?" they asked each other. "Surely we're better than her."

"My sister," said the eldest, "I think I have an idea! Let's make her stay here for more than eight days. Hopefully her Beast will be so annoyed he'll eat her."

"Very clever my dear," replied the other. "We'll do all we can to keep her here."

Having come to their evil decision the two went back into the house and acted like they were the best and most loving friends that Beauty could have.

When the time came for Beauty to leave, the sisters pretended to be utterly distraught at the prospect of her going. The sisters were so convincing that Beauty agreed to stay another eight days. However Beauty was saddened by the thought of upsetting Beast, who loved her with all his heart.

On Beauty's tenth night at her father's house she had a dream. In it she saw Beast lying on the lawn outside his palace; he was slowly dying and tears streamed down his face. Beauty woke up with a start and began to cry herself. "I am a terrible person," she said. "How could I do this to Beast, who has done so much for me? Oh why didn't I marry him? He may be ugly but he has so much more to him than that. Kindness and virtue are important and Beast has both. I may not love him, but I respect him and value his friendship. I shall go to him; he should not be unhappy. I would hate myself forever if he were.

Beauty got up, put her ring on the table and returned to bed. No sooner had she put her head on the pillow than she was asleep.

When she awoke the next morning she was
overjoyed to see that she was back in Beast's palace.
She put on the beautiful dress she found by her bed
then waited until nine o'clock for Beast to arrive.
However when the clock chimed the appointed
hour Beast did not appear. She ran around the
palace calling his name, but there was no reply.
Then she remembered her dream and dashed outside
into the garden.

There she found Beast, motionless on the grass. He
was so still she feared he was dead. Beauty threw
herself onto his body and felt for a heartbeat. He was
alive! She brought some water from a nearby stream

and gently splashed Beast's face. He opened his eyes and said to Beauty: "You forgot your promise! The sorrow of losing you made me decide to die of hunger. But in death I am content, for now I see you again."

"No my dear," replied Beauty. "You are not dead. You are alive and will be my husband. I offer you my hand. I thought that I wanted to be friends alone, but the deep sorrow that touched my heart when I thought you were dead has proved to me I love you more than as just a friend."

No sooner had Beauty finished speaking than the whole palace was lit up in dazzling light. Fireworks exploded overhead and music filled the air; but Beauty saw and heard nothing of these for she was looking at Beast, or at least where Beast had been. The monster was no longer there. In his place was a prince, as handsome as Beast had been ugly. A prince released from a terrible spell.

Beauty looked at the man lying on the grass and wondered if he could have been Beast.

"Yes, I was Beast," said the prince. "A witch cast a spell over me that turned me into a terrible monster. The spell could only be broken if a beautiful woman agreed to marry me. You were the only person who saw through the ugliness outside and saw the true goodness that lived within Beast. Now you have freed me you too are free to go. However I would prefer you to stay and be my wife and princess.

Beauty was overwhelmed. Of course, she said yes, and helped the prince to his feet. They went back to the palace and to Beauty's great surprise waiting for them was her father and all her family. The lady that Beauty had dreamt of the first time she slept at Beast's palace had brought them – she was in fact a good fairy.

"Beauty," said the fairy, "you shall be rewarded for your good character. You have chosen goodness over looks and wit. However you will now find all these qualities in your prince. You will also make a good queen; though do not forget the virtues which put you there."

Then, looking at her two sisters, the fairy said; "I know what lurks within your hearts and it is bad. I will turn you into statues, but you will be able to see and think beneath the stone that covers you. Your punishment is to see your sister in all her happiness. My spell will be broken when you are truly sorry for your behaviour. However I expect you will be statues forever as the selfish, greedy and envious are slow to see their own faults."

With a wave of her wand she transported everyone to the prince's kingdom where his subjects

were waiting. They greeted the prince and his bride
with great joy and celebration. The prince and Beauty
were married with great ceremony and their marriage
was a long and happy one.

MR SEGUIN'S GOAT

Mr Seguin had never had much luck with his goats. The same thing always happened. They chewed through their ropes and ran away to the mountains where they were eaten by the wolf. Neither Mr Seguin's kindness nor fear of the wolf was enough to make the goats stay. Goats will be goats and they like their freedom. Poor, honest Mr Seguin did not understand this and was continually dismayed.

"That's it," he said each time. "If the goats don't want to stay I won't keep them anymore."

But he always bought another one. After he had lost his tenth goat Mr Seguin bought a young one hoping that it would grow accustomed to living with him and stay.

Ah, she was such a pretty little goat too. Beautiful dark eyes, a striking white beard, striped horns, hooves so black they looked like they had been polished, and her coat was as white as chalk dust. She was very good-natured, never complaining when Mr Seguin went to milk her; nor did she try to kick the milk pail over when it was full.

At the back of Mr. Seguin's house was a field surrounded by hedgerows. This was the goat's new home. Mr Seguin fixed a stake in the middle of the meadow and fastened the goat to it, but took care to

leave a lot of rope so the goat could move about freely. He came back every now and again to see how the goat was doing and was pleased to see it happily munching on the grass.

"What a happy looking goat," he thought, "she wants for nothing!"

How wrong Mr Seguin was. His goat was bored to tears. She looked longingly at the mountains thinking, "I wish I were up there running through the heather without this rope round my neck. Donkeys and cows are let free, so why are we goats tied up?"

From this moment life in the field felt dull and insipid. Mr Seguin noticed the goat wasn't happy. She no longer produced such fine milk and she spent most of her time straining on her leash in the direction of the mountains. Mr Seguin knew she wanted something, but wasn't sure what.

One day as Mr Seguin milked the goat she turned to him and said, "Mr Seguin, I am bored here in the field. Let me take a trip up to the mountains."

"Oh, not you too!" cried Mr Seguin, knocking over the bucket in shock. He sat down in the field and asked the goat,

"So my goat, you want to leave me?"

"Yes," replied the goat.

"Won't you miss the grass here?" asked Mr Seguin.

"Oh no," replied the goat, "I won't."

"Hmm, perhaps you
are tied too tightly. Should I
lengthen the rope?" asked Mr Seguin.

"No point," replied the goat.

"Then what do you need?" asked Mr Seguin.
"What do you want?"

"I want to go to the mountains," replied the goat.

"That would not be a good idea – didn't you know there's a wolf up there?"

"I'll see it off with my horns," replied the goat.

"The wolf would laugh at your horns," said Mr Seguin. "It's eaten bigger goats than you. You don't remember the goat I used to have, a nanny goat – a big, nasty brute she was. She fought with the wolf all night but in the morning the wolf still ate her."

"Poor thing," replied the goat, "but it doesn't make any difference, I still want to got o the mountain."

"Heaven's above!" cried Mr Seguin. "What is it with my goats and their desire to be eaten? Well I will save you from yourself. In case you try to eat through your rope I'm going to shut you in the stable and you can stay there."

Mr Seguin took the goat to the stable and locked it in. Unfortunately he forgot about the window, which was open. No sooner had he turned his back than the goat escaped.

When she arrived in the mountains the goat was in heaven. Never before had the pine trees smelt so good. She felt like a queen. The chestnut trees seemed to bow down to her and the flowers opened as she passed and surrounded her in their heady perfume. The whole mountain made her feel ecstatically happy.

No rope, no stake; nothing to stop her from gambolling or grazing where she wanted. And what grass it was! Tasty, with a slight crunch and filled with thousands of different plants. Oh, the plants! So many plants and flowers that they intoxicated the goat as she dashed this way and that, rolling with her legs in the air amongst the flowers and chestnuts.

Then she jumped up onto her four legs and headed off through the bushes and undergrowth. Up the sides of mountains and down ravines she went, bellowing as loudly as she could wherever she went. Ten goats may have died up here but she was not frightened. She jumped streams, which splashed down the mountain and wet the ground all around. The goat followed one stream to the edge of a waterfall and, standing on a rock dried by the sun, took a look at the view. Far below her were the meadows and in them was Mr Seguin's house with the field behind.

The goat wept with laughter.

"How could I stay there?" she said. "It's so small!"

Oh dear. The goat had started to think she owned the world. However, all in all it was a good day for the goat. She ran this way and that, saw different birds and creatures and ate whatever took her fancy. Soon her lovely white coat was a dirty old brown colour, but that didn't worry her.

Slowly the mountains turned a soft violet colour as the evening closed in around them.

"Already!" thought the goat, caught quite by surprise at the passing of time. She looked down to the valley, but it was shrouded in fog.

Mr Seguin's fields had disappeared in the mist and all that could be seen of the house was the roof and chimney. The goat listened and could make out the noise of cowbells from the herd being brought back to the barn. Suddenly the goat felt sad.

The goat gave a start as a long howl pierced the air: "Howoooo!" It was a wolf! At the same time a horn sounded in the valley. It was the good Mr Seguin making one last effort to get the goat to come home.

"Howooo! Howooo!" cried the wolf.

"Toooooo! Toooooo!" went the horn.

The goat thought of returning, and then she remembered the stake, and the rope, and the field and decided that she preferred her new life on the

mountain. She stayed where she was. The horn stopped blowing. The goat heard a noise behind her. She turned round and saw in the shadows a pair of ears and two glittering eyes. It was the wolf! Huge, still, watching the little goat. It sat on its haunches without stirring. It knew it would eat the little goat and was in no hurry to chase it. It slowly got up with a wicked little chuckle.

"Well, hello little goat," said the wolf, licking its lips. The goat felt her world fall about her. She remembered the story of Mr Seguin's nanny goat, which fought the wolf all night only to be eaten in the morning. Perhaps it would be better to let the wolf eat her now she thought. Then the goat changed her mind. She dropped her head and pointed her horns at the wolf. She would not go without a fight. She did not think she would kill the wolf – no one had heard of a goat who had killed a wolf – she just wanted to last as long as the nanny goat.

The wolf advanced and the goat charged. That brave goat; it may have been little but its heart was big. Ten times the wolf attacked and ten times it was forced back from the fight to take a rest. And during these rests the goat would take a mouthful of grass and return to the fight with renewed spirit. The fight lasted all night.

From time to time the goat would look at the stars above her and think, "If only I could hold on until the dawn!"

One by one the stars faded from the sky. Both the goat and the wolf redoubled their efforts. The sun began to peer over the horizon…

"Finally," breathed the poor goat, who wanted nothing more than to have fought for as long as the nanny goat. With a smile the goat stretched out on the ground happy that the end was near. The wolf pounced and ate her.

THE LITTLE MATCH GIRL

I t was cold! Snow fell from the sky and the night was drawing in on this, the last evening of the old year. Through the gathering gloom walked a poor young girl; wearing nothing on her head, nothing on her feet. She had been wearing slippers when she left home, but they were no use. They were too big for a start – they used to belong to her mother – and the girl lost one when she dashed across the road. One lost and the other given to a young urchin who had much admired the slipper and had got it into his head that it would make a fine bed for any children he might have in the future.

And so the little girl walked on with her feet turning red and blue from the cold. She had a packet of matches to sell in her apron and she held some in her hand. No one had bought a match all day. She hadn't earned a single penny. Starving, frozen, what a miserable life the poor creature had! The snow fell on her golden hair, which curled around her just so; though her hair was far from her mind at the time. All the windows around her glowed invitingly and beautiful smells wafted down the street, for it was New Year's Eve.

She huddled up in a corner made by two houses and pulled her legs under her. She was so cold, but she could not go home as she hadn't sold any matches and her father would most certainly beat her for it. Anyway, it was cold at home as well, it was really only a roof over their heads; the wind whistled through the inside of the house despite the rags that had been stuffed into the cracks in the walls.

Her little hands were frozen. If only she could light one match how good that would be! If only she dared take one out of the packet, strike it against the wall and warm her fingers. She took one: striccch! How the match flared into life and burnt! It warmed her hands like a candle – what a wonderful light. The little girl imagined she was sitting in front of a great oven, so comforting was the warmth to her frozen fingers. With the cold retreating from her hands she stretched out her legs to warm her feet, but the flame spluttered and died. The young girl was left with a small burnt-out match.

She lit another match and the wall next to her seemed to become transparent, like a veil where the light fell on it. The little girl could see a table covered in a tablecloth of the purest white, on top of which was a beautiful porcelain dinner service, and a roast goose stuffed with plums and apples. And more splendid still, the goose leapt down from the table and danced across the floor, with a knife and a fork in its back, right up to the young girl. Then the match went out and the cold, dark wall returned.

She lit another match. This time she was under a fabulous Christmas tree, more impressive than anything she had seen through the windows of the rich merchants' houses. A thousand lights shone from its branches and beautiful decorations – the like of which she had only seen in the shops – gazed down on her. She stretched out her hand … and the match went out. The lights from the tree seemed to disappear upwards until the little girl saw they were, in truth, the stars in the sky. One fell leaving a brilliant tail behind it.

"Some one has just died," said the girl, for that is what her grandmother – the only one who had ever really loved her – had said whenever she saw a shooting star.

"When a star falls," she used to say, "a soul goes up the other way to God."

Again the girl lit another match. In the glow of the little flame the girl saw her beloved grandmother, happy and healthy and smiling at her.

"Grandmother!" cried the girl. "Take me with you or you'll disappear when the match goes out! You'll go just like the warm oven, the delicious goose, and the beautiful Christmas tree!"

And then she took the rest of the matches from the packet and lit them all at once! The light was so bright that it was like noon on a summer's day. The grandmother had never seemed so beautiful or so tall. She took the little girl and hugged her and they flew upwards together; happy, as they were no longer cold or hungry, with not a care in the world. They were both with God now.

And at the corner of two buildings, in the cold light of the rising sun, the little girl with rosy cheeks and smiling mouth lay dead; frozen to death on the last day of the year. A new year dawned on her small body, which still clutched a packet of burnt-out matches.

"She wanted to warm herself," the people said.

Nobody could have imagined the wonderful things that she had seen, nor would they know how happy she was now, with her grandmother, at the start of this fresh new year.

HANSEL AND GRETEL

O nce long ago, in a forest far away, there lived a poor woodcutter with his wife and two children – a boy and a girl. The boy was called Hansel and the girl was called Gretel. Now it happened that a great famine befell the land at this time and there was little to eat. Each evening the family went to bed hungry and the father was unable to sleep for worrying. He said his wife: "What are we to do? How can we feed our children when we cannot even feed ourselves?"

Terrible hunger leads to wicked plans. "I've got an idea," replied the wife. "Tomorrow, at the crack of dawn, we must take the children deep into the forest. We will build them a fire, give them each a piece of bread and then leave them. They will never be able to find their way back to the house and we shall be rid of them."

"No," replied the woodcutter, "I will not do it. How can we abandon our children in the middle of the forest? The wild beasts will devour them before the day is through."

"Idiot!" snapped the wife. "Is it better that we all die instead of just them? We must do what has to be done."

And she would not stop pestering her husband until he finally agreed to her terrible plan.

"My poor children," he wept, "my heart is now broken."

However the two parents were not the only ones awake that night. Hunger had stopped Hansel and Gretel from sleeping and they had heard every word of their cruel mother's plan. Gretel cried bitterly and said to Hansel: "We are lost!"

"Calm yourself sister," said Hansel. "Don't worry; I'll find a way of saving us."

When their parents had finally fallen asleep, Hansel pulled on his jumper and slipped out of the door. There was a bright full moon that night and its white light showed up every small stone outside the house like a shining silver coin. Hansel stuffed his packets with as many as he could. "I have a plan," he said to Gretel as he returned and both children went back to bed.

The next morning, just as the sun was hauling itself over the horizon, the wife was up waking the children: "Up you get you lazy urchins, you must come with us to find some fire wood."

She then gave them each a small piece of bread saying: "This is for your lunch, so don't eat it all now as there's nothing else."

Gretel put the bread in her apron and they all set off into the forest. Every few steps Hansel would stop and turn to look back at the house. He would then start walking again only to stop and look back again.

"What are you doing dawdling about at the back?" asked his father. "Move yourself and keep a lookout for some firewood."

"Sorry father," replied Hansel, "I was just looking at my little white kitten up on the roof. It wanted to say goodbye."

"You fool," said the mother, "that's no cat, that's the rising sun shining on the chimney."

In fact, Hansel wasn't looking for any cat. Each time he turned he was leaving a small stone on the ground.

When they reached the middle of the forest the father said: "Right, let's build a fire so you don't get cold."

Hansel and Gretel built a small pile of firewood and the father lit it. Once the fire had taken hold the children's cruel mother said: "Now that the fire's going you wait here and rest. We're going off to cut some more firewood; when we're done we'll come back and collect you."

Hansel and Gretel settled themselves by the fire and, when midday came, each ate a little bit of their bread. As they could hear the sound of their father's axe they imagined he was not far away. Little did they realise it was not the axe they heard, but a dead branch which their father had tied to a tree so it would beat each time the wind blew. Lulled by the sound the children fell asleep. When they woke it was night time.

Gretel began to cry. "How will we ever get out of this forest?" she wept.

"Don't worry," replied Hansel. "We'll wait until the moon is up and then we'll find our way home."

As soon as the moon was up Hansel took his sister by the hand. In front of them the small stones Hansel had dropped shone like silver coins, marking a trail all the way home. In no time they had returned, safe and sound. They knocked on the door, and when their cruel mother opened it she was shocked. "My poor children! Why did you spend so long in the forest – we thought you had run away," she lied.

However their father was truly glad to see them, as he never had the heart to abandon them.

It was not long before their father's joy turned, once again, to misery. Hansel and Gretel heard their parents talking: "One and a half loaves of bread," said their mother. "That's all we have left; after that, nothing. Unless we take the children back into the forest and leave them we'll all starve. There's no point all of us going hungry. You know it makes sense."

Again the father was thrown into despair. He wanted to share the bread with the children and hope something would turn up. The mother, however, was having none of it. As before she bullied and insulted the father until he agreed.

Hansel and Gretel listened very carefully. Once their parents had gone to bed, Hansel got up to fetch stones as he had done the last time. However when he tried to get out the door he found it was locked! Gretel began to cry, but Hansel comforted her. "Don't worry," he said, "I'm sure we'll think of another plan by morning."

Dawn broke and the mother roused the children from their beds. She gave each of them a small piece of bread and led them off into the forest. Along the way, Hansel dropped crumbs of his bread on the ground.

"Hansel, why are you lagging behind?" asked his father. "Come on, keep up!"

"I was just waving goodbye to the pigeon sitting on the roof," replied Hansel.

"That's not a pigeon, you idiot," said his mother, "that's the sun rising over the chimney."

But little by little, Hansel scattered all his bread along the trail.

Their mother led them deep into the forest to a place they had never been before. After building a fire she said to them: "You both look tired, why not have a little nap here while your father and I go looking for some wood for this evening. When we're finished we'll come and collect you."

When midday came Gretel shared her bread with Hansel as they sat and waited. The evening came and no one came to collect them; then the night fell and still no one had come for them. They knew then that their parents had carried out their terrible plan. Hansel said: "Well then, when the moon rises it will show us the trail of crumbs I left on the way here. We'll be home soon enough."

However when the moon finally rose Hansel and Gretel could not find a single crumb – the birds of the forest had eaten them all! "Don't worry," said Hansel, "we'll find another way home."

Though they searched this way and that they could not find their way home. All night they looked and all through the next day, but without success. By evening they were both tired and hungry and had little choice but to curl up together at the foot of a tree and go to sleep.

As dawn broke the children tried again to find their way home before they starved to death. At around midday the children spotted a beautiful white bird, the like of which they had never seen before. Its song was so beautiful Hansel and Gretel stopped to listen to it. The bird spread its wings and flew off, and the children followed it through the forest until it landed on the roof of a small house. As they approached they noticed that the house was made of sugar loaf, the roof was made of biscuit and the window frames were made of boiled sweets.

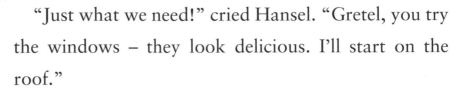

"Just what we need!" cried Hansel. "Gretel, you try the windows – they look delicious. I'll start on the roof."

Hansel climbed onto the roof and started to eat a roof tile while Gretel began munching on the edge of a windowpane. Suddenly a small voice came from the inside of the house:

"What, what, what! Who is nibbling on my house?"

The children replied:

"The wind, the wind, the wind; it's only the wind."

And they kept on eating. Hansel tore off another whole roof tile and Gretel removed a whole windowpane. Suddenly the door opened and out came an old woman. She walked with a stick and her eyes were as hard as flint. The children feared a terrible beating for what they had done. But instead the old woman said: "My dear children, what are you doing? Come on inside and stay with me awhile, and I'll look after you."

She took them both by the hand and led them into the little house. She made them a large meal and gave them plenty to drink. Full and warm for the first time in days the children felt sleepy. So the old woman made up two beds for them. As Hansel and Gretel drifted off to sleep they felt as if they were in heaven.

Unfortunately for the children appearances can be deceptive – all in the house was not as it seemed. The old woman was in fact a witch and the house was built of sweets purely to attract children. Once the witch had lured a child into her house she would kill them and eat them. Now witches don't see very well but they have an excellent sense of smell. When the witch smelled Hansel and Gretel coming she thought: "Aha, these two won't escape me. It's child-meat for my tea!"

The next morning the witch woke before the children. Seeing Hansel and Gretel asleep with their rosy red cheeks the witch thought, "Oh, what choice pieces of meat."

Then she grabbed Hansel and dragged him to a cell, which had been hidden by a screen. He was thrown in and the door was shut and locked. Next the witch woke Gretel, shouting: "Wake up lazy bones! Your brother is my prisoner. Go and make him something good for breakfast. I want him nice and fat so I can eat him!"

Gretel cried bitterly, but she still had to do as the witch commanded. While Gretel prepared the best food for Hansel all she was given to eat were the shells of prawns.

Every morning the witch went to the cell and cried: "Hansel! Let me feel your little finger – I want to see if you're plump enough to eat."

Hansel realised that the witch could not see very well, so each time she asked for his finger he passed her a bone instead. That way it never felt as if he was fat enough to eat. Four weeks passed in this fashion until the witch became tired of waiting.

"Gretel go and fetch some water for the pot," the witch shouted. "I'm going to cook Hansel tomorrow and I don't care whether he's fat or thin!"

Poor Gretel! The tears streamed down her cheeks as she went to fetch the water. "Oh, if only we had been eaten by the wild beasts of the wood," she said. "At least then we would have died together."

"Stop moaning!" snapped the old woman. "You're bleating on won't change a thing!"

The next morning Gretel placed the cauldron of water on the stove and lit the fire.

"First we'll cook the bread," said the witch, "I want the oven warm and the dough kneaded." She pushed Gretel towards the oven door. "Climb inside and tell me if it's hot enough to cook the bread."

As soon as Gretel was inside the witch planned to shut the door and cook Gretel, too. However the bright young girl realised this and said, "I don't know how to get in there."

"Oh, don't be so stupid!" said the witch. "You simply open the large door! Watch, even I can fit in there." And the witch stuck her head inside the oven. At that precise moment Gretel gave the witch a mighty heave and pushed her completely into the oven. In a flash, Gretel shut the oven. Terrible cries and horrible curses came from the witch as the flames leapt around her, but to no avail – Gretel had bolted the door.

She dashed over to Hansel's cell and unlocked the door. "Hansel, you're saved!" cried Gretel. "The witch is dead!"

Hansel flew from his cell like a bird freed from a cage. Outside the children hugged and danced, full of the joy and relief that comes from escaping certain doom. Now, with nothing to fear, they went back into the witch's house. Looking about they discovered boxes filled with pearls and precious stones.

"Now these look like useful stones," said Hansel and he filled his pockets and a bag with as many as he could carry and Gretel filled her apron likewise.

"Now it's time to leave this cursed wood as quickly as possible," Hansel said.

After a few hours of walking the children came upon a deep, broad river.

"I can't see a bridge or any boats," said Hansel. "There's no way across, we're stuck."

"We don't need a boat," said Gretel. "Look over there at that white duck. Let's ask him for help to get across.

The children called out:

"Oh duck with the beautiful white wings,

It's Hansel and Gretel!

Can you take us over the river?

We can't see a bridge."

The duck, being a kind-hearted soul, arrived at once. Hansel climbed up on its back and called for his sister to join him.

"No," said Gretel. "Together we would be too heavy. Let him take you first then he can come back and collect me."

And that was exactly what the duck did. The children set off again and soon the forest began to look more familiar to them. It did not take them long to get back home. As soon as they saw the house they dashed through the door and hugged their father. He had not had a wink of sleep since he had abandoned his children in the forest. As for his wife, she was dead – a victim of the famine which had driven them to such terrible deeds. Hansel and Gretel showed their father the precious stones they had taken and they all wept with joy at the promise of a better life.

THE MUSICIANS
OF BREMEN

A man had an ass, which had worked hard for him over the years; but was now old and tired. The man decided it was time to do away with the aged beast, but the ass, realising something was up, decided to run away. "I'll go to the city of Bremen," said the ass as he galloped off. "Perhaps there I can be a musician.

On the way he came upon an old dog lying on the ground panting, as if it had run a long way.

"Why are you panting like that?" asked the ass.

"Because I am old and weak," replied the dog. "My master was going to kill me, as I am no use to him anymore as a hunting dog, but I ran away. Oh, but now what will I do to earn my keep?"

"Listen," said the ass, "I'm off to Bremen to be a musician in the city. Why don't you come with me and we'll join a band? I'll play the lute and you can play the drums."

The dog liked the idea so they set off together. On their way they met a cat with a sad kind of look upon its face.

"What is wrong with you, dear cat?" asked the ass.

"My time is over," said the cat. "I am old and my teeth are blunt. I would rather sit by the warm stove than chase mice, so my mistress wanted to drown me. I ran away, but now what's to become of me?"

"Come to Bremen with us," said the ass and the dog. "We're going to be musicians. You can be the singer."

The cat thought that was an excellent idea and went with them. After a while our three fugitives passed by the entrance to a courtyard. There was a cockerel there that was crowing with all his might.

"You have a fine pair of lungs sir," said the ass, "What is all your noise about?"

"I was just thanking the Lord for the beautiful weather he has given us for our washing day. Not that my mistress appreciates my songs. She has threatened to give me to the cook to use in the soup."

"My red-combed friend," said the ass, "come with us to Bremen. It will be better than being made into soup! You have a lovely voice and you can sing along as we play our music."

The cockerel accepted the proposition and joined the others on the road. As they could not reach Bremen in just one day they stopped to rest the night.

The ass and the dog slept at the foot of a large tree, while the cat and the cockerel made themselves comfy on the branches. The cockerel perched at the very top of the tree, as he felt safer there. Before he went to sleep he looked in each direction, as cockerels do. In one direction he spotted a light, and shouted down to his companions that he had spotted a house. "Let's go there then," said the ass, "there's bound to be better grass there than here."

The dog mentioned that he could do with a juicy bone or two, so they set off in the direction of the light. As they got closer the light became brighter until they eventually arrived at the house. Unfortunately a gang of robbers lived there. The ass, being the largest, went to look in through the window.

"What can you see?" asked the cockerel.

"What do I see?" replied the ass. "A table weighed down with food and drink and a bunch of robbers enjoying themselves."

"That food and drink would suit us perfectly," said the cockerel.

"Indeed," replied the ass, "but how would we get in?"

They all sat down and discussed how they could get into the house and enjoy the robbers' food. Eventually they had an idea.

The ass put his front feet on the windowsill, the dog climbed on his back, the cat climbed up upon the dog and the cockerel perched on top of the cat. Then, all at once, they started to make their music. The donkey brayed, the dog howled, that cat miaowed and the cockerel crowed. At the same time they jumped through the window and landed in a big heap inside the room. The robbers, imagining they were ghosts or ghouls of some sort, leapt from their chairs and fled into the forest. The four comrades then helped themselves to the robbers' feast and ate as if they hadn't eaten for weeks.

When the four musicians had finished they extinguished the candles and looked for a place to rest for the night. The donkey found some hay to lie on, the dog lay behind the door, the cat lay in the warm cinders on the hearth and the cockerel roosted on the beams. They were all so exhausted after their long journey they were soon asleep. But they were being watched. The robbers noticed from afar that the lights had gone out and all appeared calm. The chief said: "We should not have run off as quickly as we did!" And he sent one of the men down to the house.

Finding everything quiet the man entered the kitchen. He went to light a lamp and, mistaking the cat's eyes for burning coals, approached it to get a light. The cat, believing itself to be under attack, jumped at the man and scratched him all over. The robber got the shock of his life and ran for the door. But the dog, which was lying there, jumped up and bit him on the leg. When the robber finally got into the yard the ass, which had been sleeping there on the hay, kicked him. By now the cockerel was awake, too, and let out the mightiest crow of its life.

The man high-tailed it back to his fellow robbers and said: "The house is haunted! There is a terrible witch there who spat and clawed at me with her talons. There was a man by the door who stabbed me in the leg; and there was a monster in the yard that hit me with a wooden club. And at the top of the house was a judge who shouted: 'Throw him in the dungeon!' So I rushed back here."

So the robbers never went back to the house. The musicians, however, thought it would make a fine place to stay, so stay they did; and they might still be there today.

THE EMPEROR'S NEW CLOTHES

Once upon a time there was an emperor who loved clothes so much he spent all his money on them. He was interested in nothing else, he didn't watch plays or take walks in the forests – he enjoyed showing his clothes off and you can't do that in a dark theatre or in the woods! He changed his clothes constantly; if you ever wanted to find the emperor the best place to look for him was in his changing room.

Life was pleasant enough in the large town where he lived and strangers often came to visit. One day two swindlers arrived claiming to be weavers. They said they knew how to weave the most amazing cloth you could imagine. In particular they stated they could make a cloth so incredible it seemed to be actually invisible to all but the most intelligent, tasteful, and discerning of characters.

Unfortunately the emperor lacked all those qualities, so could not see the swindlers for what they were. "I must have a suit made from such a cloth," he thought, "then I could tell who was wise and who was stupid."

He ordered a suit to be made for a grand procession and sent the so-called weavers on their way, with a huge amount of money, to begin work immediately.

The swindlers set up their looms and set to work, pretending to make the emperor his magnificent suit, calling for fine threads and sewing busily. Of course, they were really doing nothing – which they did very well – but they seemed to be working all day and in to the night.

"I'd like to know how my suit is coming on," said the emperor. Everyone in the town had already heard of the magical cloth and was eager to see it in order that they could judge who was wise and who was not too. In truth the emperor was slightly worried that he might be a bit too stupid to see the cloth. Fearing that he might appear foolish he decided to send one of his courtiers to check up on things instead.

"I'll send the old minister," thought the emperor. "His mind is sharp as a tack; I can rely on him to tell me how things are going."

So the old minister went off to see the two swindlers who appeared busy at their looms. When he saw that the looms seemed empty he was shocked.

"What on earth is going on here?" he thought; but he did not say anything.

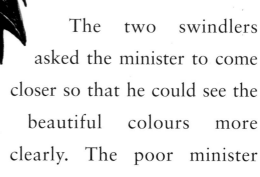

The two swindlers asked the minister to come closer so that he could see the beautiful colours more clearly. The poor minister looked as hard as he could but he couldn't see a thing; for the simple reason that there was nothing there to see. "Dear Lord," he thought, "Am I stupid? Is it possible that I am not as intelligent or as wise as I thought? I could get sacked for this!"

"Perhaps you don't see anything?" said one of the swindlers mockingly.

"What! No! I think it is wonderful!" cried the minister fixing his glasses upon his nose. "Oh yes ... those colours! The emperor will be very happy."

"We're very pleased to hear it," said the swindlers, and they talked at length about the design and colours in the cloth. The old minister tried his best to remember everything so he could tell the emperor, as it wouldn't do for anyone to think that the minister was stupid.

Then the two rogues asked for more gold and expensive threads, claiming they were necessary to finish the garments. Of course these went straight into their bags and were not used in the making of any suits or cloth at all.

Later, the emperor sent another member of his court to check on the progress of his magnificent new clothes. As before, the poor servant arrived and saw nothing, for there was nothing to see.

"Isn't it a beautiful bit of cloth?" said the swindlers and again they talked about the colours and design of their work.

"Now, I know I'm not stupid," thought the emperor's messenger. "But if I can't see the cloth perhaps I'm not as intelligent as I thought. No one shall know!" So he pretended to admire the cloth in the same way that the minister had done, telling the swindlers that the design was splendid.

"Oh yes your majesty," he told the emperor, "it is indeed most magnificent."

The wonderful new cloth was the talk of the town.

Now the emperor wanted to see the cloth for himself. He went to see the swindlers followed by all the lords, earls and dignitaries of his court. The two rascals at the looms knew of the emperor's imminent arrival so pretended to work even harder than ever.

"It's unbelievable isn't it?" said the two courtiers who the emperor had already sent. "If your majesty would take particular note of the fineness of the cloth and the splendid colours." The emperor stared at the empty looms and felt very embarrassed. "Oh how awful, I can't see a thing," he thought. "I must be a real thicko. How can I be an emperor when I'm so backward?"

But instead he said with a satisfied nod: "Oh it's wonderful. Just perfect!" The rest of his court looked at the looms and of course saw nothing. However they couldn't tell the emperor that for fear of appearing stupid – after all, if he could see it surely they could too. So instead they said to him: "Indeed your majesty, it is magnificent!"

The emperor was so pleased that everyone agreed with him on the splendid nature of the cloth that he invented the new title of "Gentlemen-weavers" for the swindlers and pinned huge medals to their chests.

On the night before the grand procession the swindlers left many lights burning in their workshop to give the impression that they were working long into the night to finish the emperor's clothes. They pretended to take the cloth off their looms and cut and sew until finally they said: "Now the suit is finished!"

The emperor and his court came to see the swindlers. The two rogues acted as if they were holding up some clothes: "Here are your trousers your majesty," said one. "And here sire, is the top and cloak," said the other. "They're very delicate, your majesty, and we warn you that they're as light as a spider's web, so you will barely know you're wearing them."

"Oooh, they do look light, don't they?" said the courtiers, though they could see nothing.

"If your majesty would be so kind as to remove his clothes," said the swindlers, "and we shall help you to put on your new suit. Then we shall have a grand unveiling in front of the large mirror."

The emperor removed his clothes and carefully put on his imaginary new suit, piece by piece. He looked down at where he believed the clothes to be, then looked at himself in the mirror.

"My, how well they fit!" said the swindlers. "The design! The colours! It's a triumph!"

The Master of Ceremonies entered.

"If it pleases your majesty, we are ready to begin the procession," he said.

"Yes, I am ready," replied the emperor. He turned this way and that in front of the mirror saying: "Don't I look wonderful!"

The courtiers, eager to seem wise, dashed to lift the hem of the emperor's cloak and stood there holding nothing but air.

So the emperor, clad in his magnificent suit, set off on the procession. The people cried from the windows, "Here comes his majesty in his new clothes! Oh how beautiful! Incredible!" And as no one wished to appear in the slightest bit stupid, each person proclaimed louder than the last how amazing the new clothes were. The emperor was overjoyed that his outfit had impressed everyone so much.

A small child's voice rang out above the crowds: "But the emperor has got no clothes on!"

"Listen to the child," said his father. And the word spread from person to person like wild fire.

"The emperor has got no clothes on," cried the people. The emperor froze. He knew immediately that they were right. But then he thought, well, there's nothing I can do, so he continued on his way, even more regally than before, his courtiers walking behind him holding up a cloak that was not there.